JOCELYN AND the BALLERINA

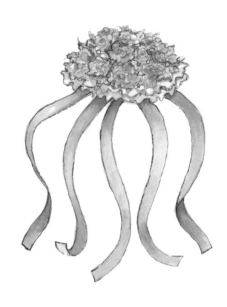

For Jocelyn Kathryn—who wore her ballerina everyday.
—XOXO Mom

For Aunty Myrna, who makes tutus
And Katherine and Anna, who make them dance.
—Linda Hendry

First published in the United States in 2000.

Fitzhenry & Whiteside acknowledges with thanks the support of the Government of Canada through its Book Publishing Industry Development Program.

Fitzhenry & Whiteside acknowledge the support of the Canada Council for the Arts for our publishing program.

Printed in Canada.
Book Design by Wycliffe Smith.

10 9 8 7 6 5 4 3 2

Canadian Cataloguing in Publication Data

Hartry, Nancy
Jocelyn and the ballerina

ISBN 1-55041-649-9

I. Hendry, Linda. II. Title.

PS8565.A673J69 2000   jC813'.54   C00-931197-1
PZ7.H37Jo 2000

JOCELYN <u>AND</u>
the BALLERINA

BY NANCY HARTRY
ILLUSTRATED BY LINDA HENDRY

Fitzhenry & Whiteside

I love my Ballerina.

Every day my mom says,
"Jocelyn, you're not wearing that old rag again,
are you?"

I pretend I do not hear.

My Ballerina hugs my legs to keep them warm.

When I dance up to the sky, the skirt twirls
'round and 'round and pushes me higher, higher.

When I go to sleep,
I shout, "Don't you dare
put my Ballerina down
the laundry chute."

I hang it on my bedpost
so I can see it
all night long.

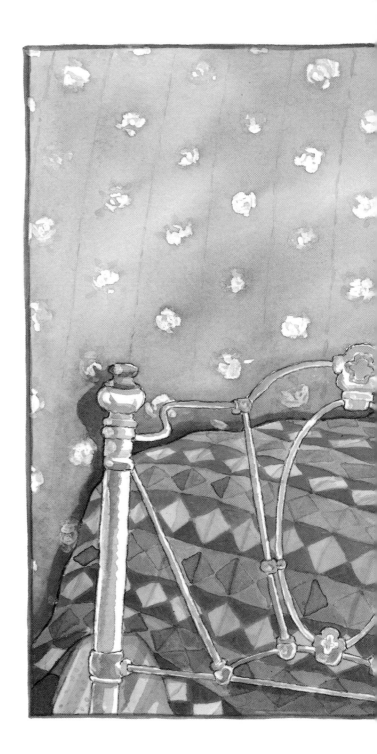

But something happens!

Every morning, I find my Ballerina
hiding under a pile of dirty clothes.

"Ta-da!" I say at breakfast time and I do
an extra special twirl.

"Oh, Jocelyn," my mom says,
"your Ballerina smells. The white has turned to gray.
It needs to be washed."

But I do not listen. My mom doesn't know anything
about Ballerinas.

"Your Ballerina is too short.
It's higher than your socks.
You have holes in the knees."

"You are right, Mom," I say.
"But I have a good idea."

I turn the Ballerina inside and out and back to front.
"Ta-da!"

I can do tricks with my Ballerina.

One day, my mom says to me, "Jocelyn, you're going to be a flower girl in Aunt Judy's wedding. I bought you a special, brand new dress.

Ta-da!"

"It is not a Ballerina," I say.

"I know, dear, but it's pink. You like pink."

"There are no leggings. It will not keep me warm."

"I know, dear. But it's summertime," says my mom.

"The skirt is not attached."

"I know, dear, but it is very pretty. I'll just hang it here on the other bedpost and you can see it all night long."

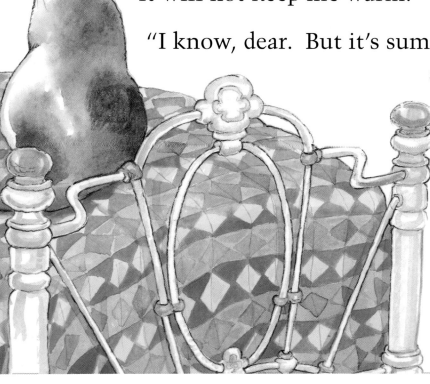

When I wake up, I am grumpy.
"How do you expect me to sleep
with that pink thing
flashing in my eyes?"

"Maybe if you tried it on,
dear, you might like it."

I pretend I do not hear.

I listen to my mom on the phone.

"We've been looking at that Ballerina every day
for six months and I'm sick of it.
If she doesn't wear her new dress to the wedding,
I'll throw the Ballerina in the garbage."

That night I put on the Pink.

I put it on the floor
and step in the middle
and pull it up.

It is lace and it is scratchy
and there are no
twirls in it.

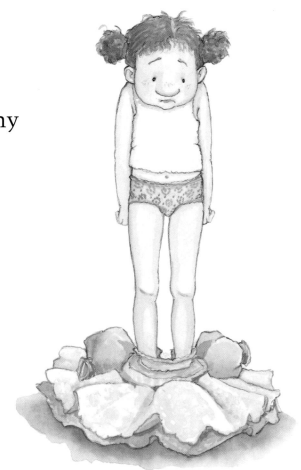

I walk down the stairs.

"Oh my, Jocelyn! You look very pretty," says my mom.

I do not look up.

On the day of the wedding,
it is cold.

"Mom—I think it will snow."

"Jocelyn, it is July."

"But, mom, the lace is scratchy."

"Jocelyn!"

I wear the Pink
to Aunt Judy's wedding.

When my mom goes to sit in the church,
I open up my purse.

I pull out my Ballerina and put it on
under the Pink.

You can hardly even see the blue stripes right through.
I roll up the legs so they don't hang down.

Aunt Judy does not know.
Mom does not know.
Just me.

I am the flower girl
so I am first.

The organ is grand,
and I am a Princess.

I hold my head up high,
and my flowers up high,
and slowly, slowly,
I step out.

Left foot.
    Right foot.
        Left foot.
           Ta-da!

Slowly,

slowly,
my Ballerina
sneaks down my leg.
Ta-da!

I can hold my flowers
in one hand and pull up
my Ballerina with the
other hand and walk,

slowly,

slowly.

I see my mom.
Her hand is over her mouth.

Aunt Judy is very happy.
She is laughing.

Silly Aunt Judy laughs so hard
she drops her flowers.

So I bend down
and pick them up for her.

Aunt Judy thanks me. The minister wipes his face with his handkerchief and then he thanks me.

I do a curtsy at the front of the church.

Ta-da!!!

My Ballerina makes the best curtsies.

It is a good thing I wore it.

I love my Ballerina.

I am going to wear it to bed.

I am going to wear it to my own wedding.

I am going to wear my Ballerina

forever.

Turn the page and find out
how to make your own bouquet.

1. Tie a small bunch of fresh or silk flowers together with a short piece of string.

2. Cut a small X in the center of two paper doilies.

3. Slide the paper doilies onto the stems of the flowers.

4. Wrap a ribbon around the stems. Attach several long ribbons at the base for streamers.